For Maria and Joe

First American edition published in 1991
by G. P. Putnam's Sons, a division of
The Putnam & Grosset Book Group, 200 Madison Avenue,
New York, NY 10016.
Simultaneously published in Great Britain
by Walker Books Limited, London.
Printed in Hong Kong.

Library of Congress Cataloging-in-Publication Data
Anholt, Laurence. What I like/Catherine and Laurence Anholt.
—1st American ed.   p.   cm.   Summary: Rhymed text and illustrations
describe a child's likes and dislikes. [1. Individuality—Fiction.
2. Stories in rhyme.]   I. Anholt, Catherine.   II. Title.
PZ8.3.A5492Wh   1991   [E]—dc20   90-27816   CIP   AC
ISBN 0-399-21863-7

1   3   5   7   9   10   8   6   4   2

First American edition

What I like

Catherine and Laurence Anholt

G. P. Putnam's Sons
New York

What I like is...

time to play

a holiday

toys

(some) boys

waking early

hair all curly

What we like is...

jumping about

giving a shout

going out

I don't like...

getting lost

I love...

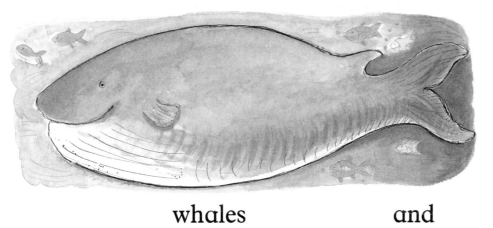

whales and snails

dogs and frogs

lots of animals

Sometimes
we don't like…

being a pair

people who stare

having to share

I hate...

thunder and lightning

I like...

playing with my mother

and my new baby brother

What I like is...

ice cream

a funny dream

my thermos flask

my monster mask

playing the fool   a swimming pool   nursery school

I don't like…

fleas

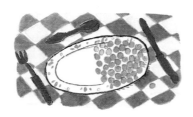

peas

bees

aches

snakes

breaks

bumps

lumps

dumps

rats

gnats

bats

What we all like is...

a Christmas tree

watching TV

a place to hide

a pony ride

let's pretend

a happy end and . . .

Making a friend.